Soaring

Soaring

Nicole Fitton

Chapeltown Books

British Library Cataloguing in Publication Data

A Record of this Publication is available from the British Library

ISBN 978-1-910542-97-2

This edition published 2023 by Chapeltown Books
Manchester, England

For my Mum

Contents

Introduction

Soaring is a collection of flash fiction short stories ranging in length and style from 70 – 1500 words. My stories are small chunks of life, perfectly wrapped and waiting for you to open!

I wrote my first piece of flash fiction in 2016. I knew I wanted to write but whether fiction or non-fiction, novels, flash fiction or short stories I wasn't really sure. I chanced upon the Screw Turn Flash Fiction Competition who were looking for stories with a ghostly theme. I'd never entered a competition nor written a ghost story for that matter. A few days later I ended up with what became *6 months, 3 Days,* a 900-word piece with a ghostly theme. I didn't win the competition but I was a semi-finalist and I received a lovely email. It was the kick start I needed and I wrote my socks off. This was followed by *Come Tilly Come*, a tale of love and loss: it was longlisted in the Exeter Short Story Competition 2016 and later went on to be included in the Arts Quarter Press' anthology *Words Catch Fire*. I was on a roll and didn't look back!

The title of this collection is "Soaring" which sums up how I feel when I write, it is also the title of one of my short stories. I do hope you enjoy my words and that in some small way they inspire you. Each story is a stand-alone piece, which can be consumed in bite size pieces until you're full!

So, whether you are on a train or a bus or simply want to read in short bursts hopefully my flash fiction stories will fit the bill. I have had tremendous fun writing them and will continue to do so alongside my full-length novels. I hope you enjoy reading them as much as I have enjoyed writing them.

Nicole

Come Tilly Come

I try hard to keep my voice steady. I want to scream *come here you naughty dog* but I don't. My cheeks are reddening; I can feel the eyes of those with perfect dogs burning holes into the back of my head. I will not turn around. A hand is placed on my shoulder. Chris is by my side, his voice calm and controlled.

'Take your time Trish, take your time.'

I take a deep breath. You had behaved perfectly all week. You had walked to heel, displaying traits of a well-trained dressage horse. I'd arrived at training hopeful.

But now, in a field full of farmers, with their perfectly trained gun dogs, the walk of shame is mine, all mine again. I'm setting a club record for having the worst behaved dog ever. You are running at the top of the field without a care in the world with your fluffy spaniel ears flapping wildly in the wind. You were perfect up until the moment you were meant to come back. I watch you go, and I'm envious. Your oblivion to my anger is total.

It has been three weeks since Tilly and I commenced our journey through the seventh circle of hell. It had seemed like a good idea when Mum had suggested it.

'It'll be good for you to get out and meet people; you can't stay cooped up forever,' she'd said, in that sage-like way only mothers have mastered.

Daniel has been gone for six months and fifteen days. Things seem slightly more bearable since Tilly arrived.

I no longer fill my time sourcing parking spaces close to the Cancer Unit, although toward the end I'd become expert at it. It was my thing, my game. It was my way of bringing normality into our fragile existence. I'd arrive at the unit early and drive once around the block eyeing up the parking possibilities before deciding on where to wait. I'd spent the best part of two years going around that car park.

If I found a space within five minutes, Dan would do well. If it took more than twenty minutes, things would be bad. Those were my rules; after all, it was my game. I even gave it a name – Car Park of Death or CPD for short!

Everyone at the unit was lovely. I didn't want them to be lovely. I wanted them to be harsh and cold and horrid. I wanted to scream and kick and punch. My first childhood fight had been in infant school with Jade Carter. She had taken my pencil case and goaded me, telling me to come and get it, laughing incessantly as I tried to grab it from her. I remember her dark eyes, staring at me, bewildered as I landed a punch square on her jaw line. I wanted the staff at the unit to be like Jade Carter. I wanted a reason to land a punch, to feel the sense of temporary relief I knew it would bring. Instead, I just smiled and said thank you for everything.

Finally, the time we'd carved out started to slow. Each day stretched into segments of waiting, regulated only by rounds of drugs and hospital appointments. Was it Tuesday? If it was Tuesday it would be a trip to see the cancer nurse. No, it was Wednesday; Wednesday was chemo day and time to play CPD!

Our friends no longer visited us. Dan was always tired or his immune system was low, or both. His eyes had sunken so far back into his head he joked he could now see life from a whole new perspective! His sense of humour was always dark and even now it was still deliciously funny.

It was towards the end of February and bitterly cold when time stood still for Dan and me. Ironically it was not the cancer but pneumonia, a secondary infection that ended our time together. He'd wanted to see the snow on the Moors. It had been such a perfect day. We sat in our Mini, wrapped in silver space blankets. We had hot water bottles and two thermoses full of tea. I'd packed your dosette box full of morphine sulphate and multi-coloured pharmaceuticals, and off we went.

Dan wore two sweaters, his now oversized favourite jeans, two pairs of socks plus a pair of bed socks, a thermal jacket, a silly woollen hat with ear flaps and the silver space blanket. He was but a remnant of the man I'd married, but I loved him more than ever that day.

With the cold biting at his bones, we made the trip. He asked me to play Queen's greatest hits and "Don't Stop Me Now" sang out as we bumped our way towards Dartmoor.

A journey started by the two of us was completed only by me. It had been bright and crisp as we sat in silence, our hands sealed together. Never before had the snow-capped Tors looked so radiant. Dan's breath became shallow and patchy. It had been his way to die, and a part of me was happy he at least got that.

As I drove us back "Another One Bites the Dust" started to play. Inappropriate? Yes, but Dan's kind of deliciously funny and I knew somewhere he was smiling at the absurdity of it all and that comforted me.

I lived in eternal winter for a while. Numb, lost and wholly unhinged. I didn't feel anything. I would wake up sweating, suffocated I think by sadness, but still, I felt nothing.

Only when mum poked her head around the door, that windy April morning, carrying you Tilly, did I feel anything. And so that is how you came into my life. You saved me that day. I should have named you naughty dog then, but I fell for your charm and named you after a sprightly old lady I had once known. I excused your bad habits, and odd smells.

It's now June and the farmers are out in force, ploughing, and planting. They eye me cautiously as I'm dragged at full pelt through their fields by a flash of liver and white fur. On Sundays, however, they are all standing in the same field as me, radiating an inner smugness. They and their obedient mutts are the crème de la crème. You and me Tilly we are called "work in progress".

The lesson won't continue until all dogs are under control. All dogs are under control, except for you!

'Call her again,' Chris encourages. I use my *I'm not mad with you* voice, as I utter that well-known call, now widely broadcast across the county…

'Come Tilly come.'

You eye me cautiously. I've been down this road before – I do not hold out much hope. But then, as if you know (you always know), you bow your head and slink towards me and sit up perfectly. I want to kiss you and smack you at the same time. Instead, I deftly slip the leash around your neck and breathe heavily. I look at you proudly. I have now joined the smug farmers club and it feels good. You look up at me, panting. Your tongue is flopping to one side in a slapstick kind of way. If you could talk I know you would say 'I did it because I could.'

Chris has offered to give us extra obedience lessons. I can hardly refuse after your Oscar-winning performance Tilly can I? At least I didn't have to jog up the muddy hill like last week so things are looking up.

For all your faults, and believe me I can recite a list as long as your tail, I love you. You listen to my ramblings, to my outbursts of anger at the complete and utter randomness of it all. I know you sense my sadness. The way you lay head down between your paws and stare up at me. When I feel as if the darkness will never lift, you nuzzle up close, your wet nose warm, reassuring me I'm not alone. I know you understand. You have fed both my heart and my soul.

Tomorrow we'll go to the beach. Dan loved the beach. We'd wander for hours breathing in its salty beauty. I wonder if you will love it too?

I shall tell you about the time we got caught out by the tide and we had to make a run for the dunes. How, somewhere along the way the car keys were lost, and how, a rotund man and his metal detector saved the day. You will pad along beside me – yes, you will be on your lead! You will give me a look that says *I'm listening intently and understanding every word, now let me off this darn lead so that I can chase whatever takes my fancy... Oh, look a seagull.*

I may think it is I training you, but we both know the truth don't we my girl?

———————

Long listed in the Exeter Short Story Competition 2016 and featured in the Arts Quarter Press Anthology *Words Catch Fire*

Amy Drake

She can still see the outline of his fingers. Patterned shades of purple and puce decorate her forearms. Their straw-coloured centres remind her of a photograph she'd once seen of a distant galaxy. His grip had been vice like and raw and the memory of it threatens to pull her into her own black hole.

She didn't really mind the bruises: it was his cheap cologne that affected her the most. It had clung to her for days. A constant reminder of her failings.

Now here she stands. He's larking around with some boys from the new estate. She smiles weakly.

'Sorry love, do I know you?' His tone is as expressionless as his face, causing his mates to stop and stare.

'Amy… Amy Drake?'

'Nay, sorry love, you'll have to remind me.' Sniggers from behind induce horror – they think it is something it's not.

The furnace within her rises and flushes out across her cheeks. *You're a bloody idiot, Amy Drake.* There is no reason he should remember her she reasons. She is just one in a long line of losers.

Eyes streaming, she turns. Her heels clip the concrete, broadcasting her departure.

Out in the bright sunlight she is exposed. Eyes sore and distended, she stops to catch her breath.

'Hay fever,' she says, to no one in particular. As if pushing the point, she blows her nose with purpose. Her fists clench and her knuckles pale. She can do ice she thinks. *Next time, next time you bastard.* She pulls out her phone and taps in her reply.

'I'm ready.'

Amy takes her time and opts for the sweetest stickiest fragrance. It is called "Fierce".

Her mum complains from the moment they leave home; Amy's perfume is giving her a headache, the roadworks are an abomination, the car is too hot, too cold. Fiddling with the electric windows for optimal blow through, Amy realises she is sharing the car with a hyperactive child. It is she who should be nervous. Closing her eyes, she sinks down into her opulently fragrant cocoon.

The hall is oppressive. The smell of unemptied bins and cheese and onion plimsoles hangs in the air. Her perfume is overpowering, and she stands, pomander like in a cupboard full of moths.

Smoothing out her drill cotton Dobok, feet bare, she waits. She adjusts the black belt coiled tightly around her like a serpent. She may as well be hung for a sheep as for a lamb she thinks.

She lands the first blow, helped by an army of forgotten souls on her back. Her technique is harsh, her speed sharp. Time passes, as first a cut to his lower lip, then a bruise to his left eye assaults him. She smiles, his wild eyes lose their focus; her perfume is working its magic.

A sting to his head, 'Amy' she whispers, a kick to his back, 'Drake' she says softly. There is no way he'll be forgetting her again.

Short List Retreat West Themed Flash Fiction Competition 2018

Mona

You can't stop staring, can you? Are my eyes following you around the room? Am I making you feel uncomfortable? Good. You should.

I was like you once. Eager to learn, the whole world at my feet. I suppose in a funny way it still is. Ironically, it is your looks of puzzlement which amuse me most.

Leo asked me the same question over and over as I sat patiently for him. I thought long and hard each time, but replied only once. He managed to capture my expression perfectly. What's that? The question? Ah, now that would be telling!

Six Months, Three Days

It's been six months, three days, not that I'm counting or anything. One minute you were here, the next you were gone. They've told me to get a grip, told me it's all in my head. They've said I should see someone, but we know the truth, don't we? You became my guardian, my protector. But it wasn't me you were protecting, was it? Is that why you left?

We had been together a while you and I, bumbling along like a pair of comfortable old slippers. I remember the first night I stayed in the house. You had scared me half to death (pardon the pun), with your banging and scratching at doors. You made my heart skip a beat but for all the wrong reasons. I felt the cold chill of your misty breath on the back of my neck. The hairs on my forearms stood tall, as I was overtaken by a never-ending wave of goose bumps that sent me into a fit of shivers. I vowed to leave, to leave and never return. Who needed a house anyway? I didn't leave though did I? You saw to that. You slammed the bedroom door tight shut, and no amount of cursing or pulling was ever going to open it. I sat in that room for hours. I was scared, but not frightened, if that makes any sense. I looked out of the back window, out over the garden. A patch of fog hung low towards the back fence, casting an unfavourable glow. For some reason it unnerved me, why, I don't know. I couldn't bear to look, yet at the same time I was completely obsessed, unable to draw myself away.

That's how it began, our connexion. As much as every bone in my body screamed for me to run, deep down I knew you meant me no harm. Even then, you were whispering your troubled siren call into my ears. You were under my skin, making me feel uneasy in my own presence. It was at that moment I knew I couldn't leave. I had to help you. I just didn't know how.

The bedroom was your domain and I respected that. It was always colder than the rest of the house. You liked it that way. It was the only room that overlooked the garden. The garden, with its magnetic pull, holding its secrets close. I know now why this had to be your room.

I noted that the fog would often settle towards the back fence. It may have been the clearest starriest night, yet a small smoke like haze would always appear and linger. I was never brave enough to venture into the garden once the fog appeared. Your room felt almost arctic when it did. Once, I'd opened the back door as the fog had started to descend. I was immediately overtaken by an irrational fear which glued me to the spot for what seemed like hours. My body had sensed something that my mind could not reconcile. I remember eventually shutting the door, I was visibly shaking. Small beads of cold sweat had formed on my forehead and I'd felt nauseous. My heart was racing irregularly. All I had done was open and close the door. Strange as it sounds, the house was too silent. It was as if a heavy blanket had been thrown on top of it. These encounters came often enough for me to grow used to them. But it was you that I was growing fond of. I felt your presence when I walked into a room and it comforted me. Our conversations were jilted at first, but we soon found a rhythm. I would talk to you and ask you questions.

You would move things or softly hit the back of my neck with an icy blast. It was enough to indicate your answer. It worked best with closed questions, yes or no answers.

Only once did you truly scare me. I had suggested you go out through the window and scare next doors children, who were erecting a tent in their garden. It was meant to be a joke. The temperature drop had been sudden and immediate. I knew it wouldn't end well for me. You threw me, with such force against the wall that I struggled to breath. Dazed, I slowly got to my feet. I was not really sure what had provoked such a bone chilling act of violence. I had somehow set the Catherine wheel spinning. Every object in the room felt your wrath that night. I'm sure the neighbours thought I suffered abuse. They looked at me with pity as I passed them on the street, but no one said a word. If they'd have asked, I would have told them the truth, but no one asked.

The gardeners came in spring. That was the beginning of the end for you and me. They had designed borders and water features. My postage stamp garden was to be transformed into a horticultural oasis. They were midway through when they came across it. A small bundle of bones wrapped in a homemade wooden box. I arrived home to find the police at my door and what looked like a CSI special being filmed in the garden. The remains were those of a small infant, dating to about 1810. They said the cause of death was most likely a fall from a first-floor window. Your spine had been broken in two places. I knew you were gone the moment I walked into the house that day. You were set free and that's exactly as it should be.

Each night I look from your bedroom window willing you to come back to me. It has been six months and three days, but you and the fog have not yet returned.

Semi Finalist in the Screw Turn Flash Fiction Competition 2016

Shoes Are Not My Only Handbag

'Look – isn't that amazing?' says Jack.

He looks at me, expecting me to understand, but I don't.

'That swan, its optimal trajectory is off; you must be able to see it?'

Not for the first time, I have absolutely no idea what he is talking about. He points to the far end of the lake where a swan skims the surface of the water. I still don't understand. I am standing beside a semi naked man who is more concerned with the flight path of a swan than freezing his bits off! What am I missing?

He turns his attention towards me. His eyes widen, his eyebrows arch ever so slightly, and the right side of his mouth slopes downward. Pools of crazy darkness burrow into me and I shift uncomfortably. The worst of it is, he doesn't know he's doing it, nor the effect it has on me.

I look down at my shoes. I'm wearing an ordinary pair of black leather loafers. Ice is beginning to replace the dew and the dampness begins to rise and invade my bones. Jack looks back to the lake. The swan has happily reached its cruising altitude and is flying off in a westerly direction. Jack gets like this sometimes – fixated. We've been here for hours. I want to be that bird, flying high above the ether, all grace and feathers. Instead at some point I've slipped once again through Alice's rabbit hole.

I find my big voice.

'Jack, we are standing at the edge of a very cold lake in December. You are hardly wearing any clothes. You're not even wearing any shoes,' I challenge, hoping he understands my concern. Whilst I enjoy our dystopian existence sometimes, I just need a little bit of normal.

'Correct, I'm not. I've told you before though, shoes are not my only handbag,' he says all matter of fact. I have absolutely no idea what that means, but I know that's the end of our conversation.

As roommates go, Jack Dubik has always been a square peg trying to become a constant circle.

We are both studying Chemistry at Bristol University. If you'd have told me I'd be sharing my digs with one of the best minds on the planet, I would not have believed you. If, however, you'd have said I'd be sharing them with a 16th century chemist, with aspirations of being Sherlock Holmes, then I would say, you've nailed him.

Jack Shepherd is brilliant and befuddling in equal measure. His view of the world is unorthodox and sometimes downright out of the box, crazy. Add in an image of a dolphin trying to learn English and I would congratulate you on your accurate portrayal! Introducing Jack to your nearest and dearest would ultimately result in disinheritance, not to mention the need for powerful prescription drugs. Jack will do and say whatever takes his fancy. He can be harsh and lovely in equal measure.

In the two years we have known each other, I have been arrested for affray, eaten my weight in crickets and been convinced that Jack Shepherd is the next stage in our evolution. In my defence, I would like to argue that on each occasion, large quantities of alcohol had been consumed.

I remember the day Jack and I met. He'd been sitting alone in the canteen. He'd looked hungry and lost so I shared my lunch with him and that is how we began. Slowly and unexpectedly, he captured my heart.

His upbringing had been somewhat unconventional. At the age of seven he'd been sent by his parents to "find himself". He had taken his five-year-old sister along with him. They were dropped off in a forest and given a map. They'd made it home six hours later and had covered a distance of over twenty miles. Nowadays his upbringing would be called neglect or abuse or something. You could argue he's the way he is because of it; that it's given him an alternative slant on life, but I would disagree. His sister Milly is not seven shades of crazy. She's an accountant. Jack is wired differently that's all. Our life together is never dull or verbose. It is disjointed and surreal and moves at breakneck speed, but it is never boring.

Over the last week or so his episodes have become more frequent and intense. Yesterday I found him with his head inside the oven. My heart stopped until I remembered it was electric! He'd been trying to create rain clouds and lightning within the confines of a student kitchen cooker using static electricity. It is no wonder that our three-bedroom flat only has two occupants! It is like living in close proximity to a wild animal. My heart carries a different set of beats when I'm with him and it's exhilarating. I catch a glimpse of the world through his eyes and everything makes sense, in a weird sort of way. He is of course completely mad. But that's OK, I'm not sure I like normal anymore.

I awake to find Jack gone. I am exhausted but refuse to give in to the years of tiredness that are swilling across my soul. As usual he's left the front door wide open and I catch a whiff of Andres all night kebab bar and grill. It's a good job this is Bristol and not Beirut! I check the time – 5.30am. My phone blips.

'Clifton' is all the text message says. My heart sinks. Not now, not today, please not today. I have a paper to submit. My tutors can smell my imminent failure. If I ignore him, he won't understand, if I go to him, he won't understand. I'm stuck. Slowly I pull on my trousers. I can see my breath in front of my face and hurriedly search for the thermal vest my mum so thoughtfully sent me. My phone beeps again.

'I'm waiting.'

Bloody hell this had better be good. I slam the door behind me and head for the suspension bridge.

Jack is looking out across the Avon Gorge some 245 foot below. There is little traffic this time of the morning and the lights twinkling from the bridge give it an ethereal quality. It seems fitting that this is where he's chosen. This week he's been working on a supersonic particle experiment. Clifton is where the last ever Concorde flew. He is animated, and his arms gesticulate enthusiastically. I'm not convinced he's aware I'm even there. I'm cold and tired and seriously jeopardising my future. At that moment, he turns toward me. His wild eyes know what I'm thinking and I feel guilty.

'This is it, James, this is the big one. I'm going to put Newton's Third Law of Motion to the test,' he says.

I nod. I have no idea.

He is carrying a large purple handbag containing all manner of chemical wizardry, a pair of black patent court shoes, a silk scarf and what appears to be an assortment of kindling. The poor night bus driver must have had kittens.

'Can we go now, I'm freezing?'

I move from foot to foot as if to emphasise my point. Jack has stopped and is giving me that look. He is the grand master and I am the rooky.

'You go, I need to finish this.'

I walk away, confused but no more so than usual. I listen as his voice fades and I begin to warm up. He drives me crazy, but I love him unconditionally. I know he will never reciprocate, but I love him just the same.

I never did pluck up the courage to tell him. I'm not sure he would have understood. He didn't really do emotions.

As we carry the small wooden box into the church, I half expect him to leap out and give me that look of disappointment he had crafted so well.

You did it my gorgeously beautiful friend, you did it. You launched yourself into space and left me as usual to pick up the pieces. Later today Milly and I shall take you on your final mission.

We stand on Clifton Suspension Bridge. It feels strangely empty. It is a perfect night, all crisp and bright with the North Star in ascendance. Milly hands me the sealed cardboard tube attached to our homemade rocket and I kiss the tube fondly. We have drawn our own epitaphs in big felt tip pens. Milly has drawn a pair of fine-looking shoes; I have drawn an accompanying sky-blue handbag with your initials – J.A.S. We watch, as you climb high into the inky canopy. I can't think of a word to say. I shall miss you deeply but I know you'll be at your happiest amongst the stars.

Thunder Song

Leah wasn't sure how long she'd sat in the shadows. Walled by the darkness, she listened as the music played on repeat. Her damp bony fingers made staccato moves and stabbed at the air keeping time on an imaginary keyboard.

She could hear the tremor held at the edge of his voice, distant and haunting. His words ran 33 1/3, needle to grave, released momentarily to cut the air before being absorbed back into the blackness of the vinyl. It had been his biggest hit and her biggest shiner. The song was written the day he'd signed the contract, the day her world changed, and the impact of his words slammed every door shut. Every bottle of vodka breached, every excuse given, but an empty bottle was still hollow no matter how hard you hit it against the wall.

Leah lifted the needle from the record and replaced it delicately back into its cradle. His eyes were like thunder, and his dark words rumbled close and exploded around her. Like stones thrown at glass they were unforgiving, and she shattered.

Years later she would find pieces of herself reflecting up from the floor. She would think of butterflies and pancakes but not once of him. The piece that made sense of it all was never found. It lay lodged under the fridge, visible only in the half-light. The tile to complete her nine-letter word was hidden for all eternity. She'd always been crap at Scrabble.

Leah lengthened her hands out in front of her. Funny things hands she thought, best when kept busy, out of trouble. Could a song only half written still be called a song she wondered? She wanted to be more than just the chorus.

Leah slipped the record back into its sleeve and placed it on top of her stacked clothes and dog-eared diet books. She wiped the blade clean and buried it between freshly laundered socks and faded denim. Shutting the suitcase, she closed the door softly behind her.

———————

Featured on *Reflex Fiction* May 2019

A Moonless Sky

March ~ 1645

I feel the rope tighten around my wrists. Leon is behind me, and I can smell his stale body odour, all sour and bitter. His hair is as wild as his eyes, and the fear behind them is clear and present. Brainwashed whispers and wooden crosses have bent him backward, and I no longer see the man I thought I knew.

Witchcraft is said to be about these islands, blown in on a dark tide its remnant seeps beneath our doors, always cold, always afeared. Since the day I first drew breath, I have known of its power as fires in grates across the island burned both day and night, and strings of bitter herbs swayed from every timber frame in an attempt at reassurance.

I am no more wicked than a goat or a chicken yet I am called Sorceress. It is but one man I did ensnare by nothing more than the innocence of love, yet now he ties my hands and binds my feet, and I realise with sadness that his love for me meant no more than froth upon a wave.

The only evidence brought against me is a fancy of string and feathers which I'd hung above my bed. Now it is a sign of my guilt, a caster of spells. I'd picked heather to brighten my small home without a thought of how things so innocent would seal my fate.

September ~ 1644

Mary speaks of days I do not recognise, when natures laws healed and provided comfort. She had known my mother all of her life. We are gathering seaweed on the shoreline and salt pricks at my cracked lips, making me smart.

'My mother was a good woman, Mary, but goodness mattered not a jot, it was all lies Mary,' I say.

'Aye, child, but lies or truth it makes no difference when you have the crown on your side, your father knew that,' she says softly.

I nod. Only on my father's passing did I fully comprehend the depth of his love and the extent of the pain he carried.

'Your mother did not need a new God to worship. Her Gods were the sea and the land,' she says looking out across the ocean.

'Your father begged her to conceal herself, just until the new order settled, but she could not. The truth was as ingrained in her as patterns in wood.'

My tears begin to fall and Mary takes my hand.

'They burned her and were it not for your father's faithful service to the crown they would have taken you too.'

Sadness fills the space between us and instinctively I wrap my arms around my belly.

'With my father gone, they will come for us?'

I already know the answer before the words even leave my lips.

'You are her daughter, right enough. They will be afraid, especially when they know you are with child.'

'Afraid they should be,' I say simply.

'Then be ye prepared girl for they are as cunning as pirates and twice as deadly.'

My daughter is born beneath a moonless sky, to the sound of fierce waves crashing against a silent beach. I lie for hours marvelling at her small hands and cherry red hair. As I look into her dark eyes, I see a thousand twinkling stars and know what I must do.

A soft knock on the hard door catches me, and for a moment, I freeze.

'Faye, it's me, open the door.'

I do not hesitate and fling the door wide. It is a voice I have longed to hear. Leon will see our beautiful daughter, take my hand, and all will be well.

I notice the mist which clings to his hair before I see the unease which rests in his face. In the half-light, he looks caught, like the moment when you fall beneath the waves, and the world is all stillness and calm before the panic sets in, and the thrashing begins.

'You need to leave Faye,' he says. No hello, no request for forgiveness.

'Are you not to come in and warm yourself?' I ask, stilling my excited heart against the frame of the door. But I know even before he shakes his head that I have lost him. Somewhere between our love lost days and whispered promises, he has betrayed me.

'What has happened to you, Leon?' I ask. 'What have they done to you?'

There is a hesitation, a trace of something, but it is gone before I can decipher its meaning.

'They will come for you, Faye, for you and the…' His feet shuffle, and his eyes unbundle scattering left and right.

'It's just me,' I say quickly and pray that my precious secret does not wail and reveal my lie. Leon's eyes flicker unconvinced, but he does not push me. The wooden cross around his neck is something new, and I bite my lip and hold in my anger.

'It's as well the baby did not survive,' are his parting words. I stand and watch his form grow smaller; he does not turn back.

Taking the back path, I move quickly across stiles and swollen streams. It is the Sabbath, and not a soul will dare to venture out before church. I turn and see the rain sweeping in toward our distant home. A line of red dots are moving toward our small cottage, like a string of fiery caterpillars. The fire within their well-oiled torches will be no match for the approaching storm, and I smile. I rest and watch my beautiful daughter sleep, and as night approaches on silent feet, I steal away to the far west of the island where the three seas meet and the ancient ways both dark and light secretly thrive.

March ~ 1645

In the split breath, before the tinder catches, I am at peace. For six months they had searched for me finding nothing more than rumours and shadows. My daughter's safety is now secured, and I have returned, defiant and unyielding. After my mother's murder I retreated from my path, believing all faults to be within, but their words never reached my heart and like oil across water they trickled down my back and pooled at my feet. If I had not already lived the life for which I was born I would have stood my ground and challenged and pushed and charged.

My daughter carries within her a soul strong enough to tear down the armies of Hades; there is nothing I can add save my sacrifice to stoke an already bubbling revolution. While eyes are turned on my flicker and flame my daughter will grow in peace, unknown to anyone outside of Mary and the elders.

With the little movement I have left I beckon Leon toward me. His apprehension is palpable and although I am the one tied to the stake; he is the one who looks afeared.

'What do you want witch?' he spits.

His angry words have caught the attention of the gathering crowd whose murmurs rise.

'Closer,' I say and Leon shuffles a little closer.

'She's coming Leon, on wings that look as fragile as birdsong but are as deadly as poison, she is coming. Like a hungry crow, she will hunt for you and peck out your eyes.'

Leon turns away sharply, but before I can catch his eye the flames rise and I begin to dissolve into a thousand pieces.

I feel myself unshackle; it is a welcome release, and I am not afraid of any of it. I am but a branch, and the roots of my heritage are mined deep. The island shall return to the old ways, and I shall live through my daughter as my mother has lived through me.

From a faraway hilltop, Mary watches as distant smoke dances across the early evening sky. In her arms is Veronica, a child born of love and magic. Behind them stands a legion, hidden in spring mists and high tides.

Before the dawning of a new day, the islanders will no longer doubt the existence of magic, and a young girl born beneath a moonless sky shall direct both the light and the dark.

———————————

Short listed in the Exeter Short Story Competition 2020

I Don't Want to Dance

I don't want to dance. Dancing is for wussies. All those limbs to coordinate, no thank you very much. I am happy to sit in my high tower and look down on the dreadfulness of it all. No, dancing is not for me. There really can be no excuse for wanting to look that foolish in public. Anyone over the age of thirty should not be so free and easy with their pelvis – fact. I cast my eyes across the crowded dance floor and slowly shake my head.

Something very strange seems to happen when people attend celebratory functions. All propriety disappears and people just behave differently. I don't like it. It's not normal, it's totally weird.

Dancing makes me think of that song by Eddie Grant. I sit on my hands in defiance. I am not shaking my bootie, not even to a top tune like that – I don't wanna dance, not now, not ever baby!

Seeing Mum and Dad dance has made this officially one of the worst days of my life. It is up there with pet death. I don't want to look, but my gaze refuses to avert. Whoever told my parents they could dance should be shot and their innards should be removed with a teaspoon. They have a style that does not so much shout "slave to the rhythm" as "stampede of the rhinos". Dad is busting shapes that come from a different planet. I just wish it was on the other side of Jupiter.

Out of the corner of my eye, I catch a glimpse of Uncle Barry. He is out of his seat faster than a greyhound out of its trap. He's all teeth and trousers.

His hips are swaying vigorously from side to side. Someone needs to warn the NHS – they're gonna be busy later.

'Do you want to dance?'

'No, thank you.'

Go to hell, is what I want to say. I smile politely. Mia Woods shrugs her shoulders and wanders back towards the bar. There is no way that Mia Woods will ever convince me to forgo my self-respect. *I said oops upside ya head, I said oops upside your head…* What sort of living hell is this? I don't think I've been this embarrassed since Mum turned up at the school fayre with a packet of Tesco's value cupcakes labelled "homemade".

Why can't I have a normal family like the one Natalie Andrews has? Her mum shops at Waitrose and drives an Audi. I'd be happy living in that family. I'd be happy with Natalie Andrews too!

'Are you sure you don't want to dance?' Mia Woods is back.

'No, thank you.'

I smile, not so politely this time. Mia's face says everything evil, but her lips don't move. She wears her scowl well and turns away. I always thought she was smart – obviously not.

My sister Philippa, is now dancing with dad. Watch out Ed Balls, there's a new kid on the block. Mum flops down beside me. She looks exhausted and her mascara has decided to migrate south. It's not a good look, I really should tell her.

'Are you OK love?'

She looks concerned, in a freakish sort of way.

'Why don't you get up and dance, it'll be The Spice Girls next?'

'I don't like The Spice Girls,' I say.

'Oh, come on Charlie, everyone likes The Spice Girls... even your dad likes them.'

Surely, she must know that citing Dad is not a good endorsement?

I glare at her, giving her the full benefit of my pout sulk. I pierce my lips together tightly and blow air forwards. I've practiced it in the bathroom mirror. It makes me look like a duck, but it's still better than looking like a wally on the dance floor. If they'd have made the pout sulk a GCSE I'd get an A* no problem. Mum takes the hint and heads back to the dance floor. Her sparkling shoes dangle loosely in her right hand. I watch as she weaves first left, then right. Occasionally her foot seems to get stuck on a floor tile, throwing her ever so slightly off balance. If I didn't know better, I'd say she was on the deck of a ship. I know, it's sad. Imaginary ships and drunken mothers – whatever next? I wonder how I can possibly be related to these people.

Uncle Tony is pissed again. The lure of a free bar has proved too much. Concentric cycles of sweat have formed under the arms of his lilac shirt. With his arms raised high above his head, he claps to a random beat that only he can hear. Surely, it's time to leave now, please someone say we're leaving?

They haven't even cut the bloody cake! I stare down at the confetti-strewn table. I wish the horseshoes were real and life-sized. I could do some serious damage. Natalie Andrews would die of shame if she were here. All this compulsory frivolity and bodily contact – yuk. Everyone is trying too hard. I want things to go back to how they should be. I miss the sarcastic comments between Dad and Uncle Barry and the death stares between mum and aunty Maxine. All this lovie lovie stuff is doing my head in. Everyone seems to have amnesia. I want to shout *we loathe each other, remember?* I'm struggling with all this getting along malarkey. I think I'll be eternally scarred. It may well be the happiest day of Simon and Debbie's life, but it the most profoundly disturbing day of mine.

'Do you want to dance?'

Oh, sweet Jesus, when will she give up?

'No, thank you.'

I really don't know how many times I can say it. I have never really considered murder before. Like proper, real life, blood and everything kind of murder… until now. This time I don't smile. This time she gets the full-on pout sulk. Mia starts to walk across the room towards my brother – finally, hallelujah!

I can tell from Henry's posture that he has accepted the challenge. Entertainment at last! I fumble for my phone; I need to capture every agonising, belly laughing moment. Maybe, just maybe, this wedding isn't so bad after all.

The evening "do", with cold finger buffet and vegetable shaped flowers is about to commence and heralds yet more arrivals. Henry is sacrificing sausage rolls and limp quiche triangles. Blimey, this shit just got real.

I move swiftly around the dance floor, being careful not to step into the path of its magnetic field. The sticky outer edging hampers my progress and makes me walk in a disjointed stop-start sort of way. I too have entered the invisible ship. Henry has metamorphosed. His feet have gone all John Travolta. Thank you Take That, your harmonies shall not be forgotten. Henry's fire has been relit. Even the gannets at the buffet have stopped and are staring wide-eyed at such a fine display. I stand on my chair, but it's no use. The crowd surrounding them has swelled to epic proportions. I scurry in between dad and Aunty Maxine. I want to capture every breath-taking moment in full technicolour. It is a performance worthy of YouTube. Thank you, little brother – I am on the road to making my millions.

Three and a half minutes is not long enough. Rapturous applause ensues. Henry takes a bow and even Mia is clapping respectfully. I pull out my baseball cap from my jacket pocket and pass it around. Well, why not? Mum is always telling me to be "creative". Mum puts her drunken arms around me.

'Wasn't your brother brilliant Charlie, wasn't he just bloody brilliant?'

'Yes mum, bloody brilliant.'

My baseball cap is weaving in and out; it looks heavy. I'm starting to feel happy. I unhook myself from mum's sweaty grasp. I really should tell her she looks like a panda. If I had a match right now, I bet I could set her on fire. She must be breaking some sort of EU emission laws. I've lost sight of my cap. Oh no, surely no one would nick it, would they?

'Have you seen your dad?' Mum asks.

'I think he's outside with Aunty Maxine.'

'Oh, is he now.'

It is enough to get her firing on all cylinders and heading off in the direction of the garden. Finally, things might be getting back to normal.

I look across the room and my heart stops. A sick feeling is rising in my chest. Natalie Andrews with her long brown hair and perfect skin is here, she's here! Natalie Andrews and her textbook family are here at my family wedding. She waves and beckons me over. She is so beautiful.

'Hey!'

'Hey,' I shout above the music; I am so uncool it's embarrassing. I can't stop staring at her.

'Do you want to dance, I love dancing, don't you?'

I nod enthusiastically. 'Yea I love dancing' I say.

Soaring

I feel the wind rush past my ears as I climb. I recognise the town below; it's different to the London I know, but, London it most certainly is. It's always London.

My arms are pinned to my side as I rise higher and higher. I feel the sharp drop in temperature; an icy chill explores my face as I continue my ascent. I must be at about 25,000 feet by now. I know what's to come and I savour it; the anticipation is biting at my lips. My speed slows, and the tension held within my torpedo like frame lessens. Slowly, with weightless ease, my arms start to unfurl from my body. They fan out from my sides as I start to negotiate my descent. I ride each thermal buoyantly. I am connected to the opulent luxury that has been afforded to me. I'm as a feather thrown by the wind. I know not the way of my passage tonight, I am grateful only for my escape. I tip a wink to the stars and the moon. This is my heaven, my sanctuary. I ebb and flow, up and down, left and right. I am free, directed only by the breeze. Tonight, it's an easterly, light and fluffy, allowing for smooth aerial transitions. It allows me to glide, a skater on a sky full of invisible ice. I slowly spiral downwards, large open perfect spirals. I'm down to about 8,000 feet now.

I can make out the people below. I see a land full of matchstick men and matchstick cats and dogs. I watch as they frenetically weave, negotiating with the inevitability of life. I feel nourished by my invisibility. I scream and shout, hearing my voice resonate across the clouds; I feel glorious. The world below seems small, insignificant. The truth is, we are all small and insignificant. I turn my attention to the traffic. It never ceases to amuse me. Stop, start, quick, slow; real world bumper cars in an unreal world. The traffic is as constant as the force that greets me each morning, and I shudder. They are unaware of my presence; they do not feel what I feel. How can they? They are trapped by their own gravity. It has them chained, grinding them into a life of so called purpose. As I soar through the clouds I am alive, for now anyway. The night will soon draw to a close. Passing quickly, it will give way to my harsh existence. For now, though, that truth is held down firmly by gravity, so, I continue to soar across the moonlit sky.

Daylight beckons. I start to feel the heat of the sun; it's pulling me back. My yoke, once again is firmly reapplied. My wings have healed me; they have saved me for another day. Up high I am free from his smoke-filled kisses, and his vice like hold. I'm at liberty to have my own thoughts and my own dreams. He will be gone when I awake, ashamed and riddled with guilt. It won't last long though, it never does. The heat of this arid land will once more take hold; it's burnt ochre hues and oppressive heat confirm I am indeed awake. My unseen chains of bondage will again shine bright. I have become an expert of disguise. I will step back into my world of possession. I will again become the loving wife, the respectful daughter. I am convinced nobody knows my name. I'm called diligent and dutiful. I am never Naomi. My name holds too much power; it sings of strength and defiance. No, my name would be a sign he cared, it would be harder for the whip to fall on Naomi. I cleverly excuse my bruises, but on the inside, they burn like molten lava. We were a good match for both families. There is no doubt we look good on paper.

As nights shadow starts to fall, I am gripped with a fear that is my own mortality. It screams silently for me to run, but to where? Will tonight be the night it ends? I hear the door close and watch as his mask slips and falls. It drops as a stone into a pond.

I will the hours to pass. I do not understand. I will never understand. His arm will fall across my face and again it will begin. He is a man of only one season. The egg shells on which I walk cut deep into my soul. I struggle to outwardly display an air of nonchalance. Shards of wretchedness twist in my lungs and I inhale sharply. I am aware that this very act of defiance may have repercussions. From the corner of my eye I watch the clock. I keep my eyes permanently fixed on its hands. Listening to its gentle tick, tick, tick. I am unwilling to avert my gaze. If I look for long enough the time will pass. It makes no difference what I think or feel, all that matters is that I am here. My head begins to feel unclear and my perception of light starts to dim. My blood no longer flows freely. It has reached the stage of coagulation. I am fully immersed in a performance of survival. I need to survive just one more night. I immediately banish the thought from my head, I cannot risk discovery.

As quickly as it begins, it ends. I listen not moving, his alcohol fuelled frame, shuffles and stumbles towards the TV. Here he will stay until morning.

I greet the cool water on my face as a welcome friend. It signals a change of pace and I can begin to breathe again. My time to reign supreme is almost upon me. I lock the bedroom door and embrace the freedom sleep affords me.

As I drift, I unshackle. I discard the name that is tied like a lead weight to my humanity. It can no longer force me to the depths of those cold dark places and, I start to climb. I taste the low-level mist as it catches on my tongue and I continue my ascent. I am resplendent and whole. My beloved London is laid out below me, a display of the finest jewels sparkling in the autumn evening. I am soaring higher than before. I'm at the limit of my existence and it is magnificent. This is my world now. High above familiar streets I listen to the ease of it all, a lullaby calling me home. I am sleeping deeply, but, I am more awake than I've ever been. I am negotiating my survival in my one safe place. This may be my last night in my world of clouds and hope. I ebb and flow, marvelling at the enormity of it all. Sadness grips me, as the thought of not returning crosses my mind. You came to me, when I thought all was lost you found me, broken, despair biting at my bones. You lifted me above the clouds, giving me the courage to think "what if?" For that I am eternally grateful.

Tomorrow everything will change. I try not to think of it too much. I do not want to raise any suspicions I shall be running for my life, it will be terrifying but glorious. For now, I drink in the beauty of the night. I am like an excited child the night before Christmas.

I breathe broad and deep. A conscious desire to belong to this world has begun to invade my soul. I dare to believe I have a place on this earth. Soft white clouds once more envelope me. I look out of the cabin window of the 747. Its engines propel me forward. I am inching towards a coveted commonplace existence. I am returning namelessly to my beloved London, and it feels miraculous. The warmth of my mother's hand a reminder I have truly escaped. I peer longingly out of the window. I do not ache for my life of woe, but for the beauty and equanimity the night gave to me. The night with its many shades of dark indigo and crystal stars, called me into the safety of its presence. I feel my wings softly detach and, stroking my back they bid me farewell. As I continue to gaze a figure too small to define ghosts into view. I squint and see the shape swoop and dive through a distant bank of clouds but… Surely it can't be? My eyes start to flicker, the weight of the day hangs heavy upon them, and I blink. The figure is gone. I lie back in my seat and smile for the first time in years.

Short listed for the Black Pear Press Short Story Competition 2016

Salad Days

Abdomen exposed, his desire to find a new home is strong and desperate. No more kicks or punches taken on a bed of cardboard and newspaper.

He moves across town, first left then right. A doorway, a bench hidden by undergrowth, a stretch of urine-soaked wall beneath a glowing shop front. But none are right and time is running out. Like a Hermit crab in search of a new shell, Theo explores the darkest of corners.

His search takes him out of town and down to the shoreline where the breeze is salty and space is no longer a premium.

Brightly coloured boxes sit like strings of pearls against a backdrop of sand. Inside, a kettle, a half-eaten crab sandwich. Theo unties the bundle from his back. A ring, a photograph. He redresses his wounds packing them tight, and sleeps for all eternity.

———————

Featured in *Ad Hoc Fiction* May 2019

Jellied Eels

Tom lights his cigarette and inhales deeply. It's the last in the packet. It'll probably be his last for a while. Supplies have run short, who knows when the next consignment will manage to get through. He wipes the sweat that's pricking across the surface of his forehead with his bandaged hand. Only two fingers missing, he can still hold and fire a gun they told him cheerfully. As if that's any consolation. When he gets home, if he gets home, he'll be needing to milk the bloody cows, that's if there's anything left to milk. Tom looks down at his hand. He doesn't feel as if he's lost his fingers, they still feel as if they're there. Maybe in the panic the doctors got it wrong. The chap next to him was in a bad way, maybe they've made a mistake. The chap next to him didn't have any arms, no, there was no mistake.

The water today is lower than yesterday. Yesterday it came up as high as his knees, today it only reaches as far as his calves. Tom stares down at the dark brown mirk. Each step reminds him of walking on fresh wet sand just as the tides gone out. If he stands still too long, he'll get stuck. The captain doesn't appreciate having to come and rescue some poor private sinking further down into the slimy depths. 'You'd wish the Jerries had got you son' the sergeant had said. Tom didn't think he'd want the Jerries or the captain to get him. Some of the chaps joke and say there are eels swimming around in the murky depths. He wishes there were, it would make a change from Maconochies Meat Stew and hard biscuits. The thought of a large helping of jellied eels makes his mouth water and he swallows hard. The guns have been silent this past hour or so. Soon they will begin again. Jerry doesn't stay silent for long. Soon their trip trip trip and deafening booms will fill the air, obliterating the ability to think clearly. Those are the times he likes least, swilling around in his own private hell bath. He doesn't want time to think. Thinking unnerves him, makes him edgy. Much better to be doing. What is it the captain says – *An idle soldier is a dead soldier.* No, he'll be no good dead. He'd definitely get a wallop from his mum if he wound up dead. Being anything other than alive was not an option. Tom looks out across no man's land. Even though the firing has ceased a grey mist hangs low across the field. The moon is now up, glints of sparkling diamonds sing out from the field.

He feels something brush passed his right leg. It's too long to be a rat. He turns sharply. The lads think it's funny. Tom doesn't think it's funny. He thinks it's bloody rude teasing him like that. He makes a note to speak to the sergeant. Just because he's the youngest doesn't mean he should be the butt of their jokes. They have stopped laughing and are staring past him. He's not going to fall for it. He starts to move toward them and their expressions hold. They have all run atop the sand bags, their faces look ashen even in the dim twilight. Old Harry is standing on a chair and Tom wonders how long it will hold bearing the weight of an old codger like him.

Something pushes against his left leg, this time with a lot more force than before. His leg bows under the pressure and he almost falls head first into the murky depths. He feels his pulse quicken. He knows that feeling well. It reminds him of home, of days spent in and out of the river. He smiles and licks his lips. It looks like he may just get his wish after all.

New Shoes for Christmas

Pieces of his imagination capture my soul as I sleep, and I am awoken abruptly feeling its loss. He holds it to ransom. *It'll cost you more than a penny to get it back laddie*, he whispers. He seals the box tight and places it on the table at the end of the bed. I can't see it clearly, but somehow, I know it's there. Escape is not promised, but I'll do my best.

I can see it clearer now. Bathed in light beyond the crisp linen and white noise its shape has formed and I hold it in my mind's eye. The roadmap to my future is translucent and hollow. At that moment I want to make it out more than anything in the world. I calculate the distance and imagine my journey all stretched and elongated, as though it's there but not there, like a 3D hologram or a ghost. I wobble not convinced I possess enough strength or courage. At times everything is in sharp focus, and I know what I need to do. I need to push forward, head first, arm raised like Superman and project myself towards the end of the bed. But just when I think I've got the hang of things, just when I'm starting to make progress, I'm pulled back tighter than a big dog on a short leash. The keeper of my soul has waged war against me, and it's up to me to fight back in this game of life.

Stretched sheets bind my feet. My skin is sealed within a cotton shell. A bedtime tortilla with a live filling. My arms try to lengthen, and I dig my small nails into the Egyptian cotton. I am hanging on but only just. For a moment I lose sight of him, and my eyes flicker. *Now then big man, ya did nay think I'd leave ya did ye?* I try to shake my head, but only my mind moves. I am moving towards the end of the bed now, voices around me chime and chirp. It's a lesson in forced fun as no one is sure if I'll survive the night. But tonight, my eyes will be out on storks, lollipops from Willy Wonka's chocolate factory, I will not drift off to the land of Nod, but I will survive. I know I will always be my brother's keeper.

A week overdue was not part of her birthing plan; there was no column for plan B. She was as prepared as a pastor's wife needed to be. Martha had thought of classical music and birthing pools; of candles and soft scents. Her husband called on all that was holy, and a prayer chain the length of Britain mobilised. But fourteen days in and the good Lord had turned a deaf ear – babies? What babies, I don't know about any babies.

Bean bags were replaced with stirrups and hot curries with gas and air. Any notions she still held of a natural delivery withered and her dreams exited as day fifteen dawned. Pastor Pete proclaimed a message of hope, and she threw up all over his brogues. Contractions refused to come, and shoeless Pete knelt at every given moment. Martha would bargain with the devil if it meant she could fit back into normal knickers again.

Complications they said as they wheeled in the incubators and placed them at the end of the bed. Martha felt small and vulnerable. Dull rhythmic sounds pulsed and pinged. A circle of mechanical prayer surrounded her – each wire a voice, each light a beacon.

'We'll take it from here, Pastor,' they said as Pete was shouldered gently from the room. Secretly she was relieved. A chorus of artificial heartbeats peeled around the room and the bright white lights focussed in at the business end. Martha thought of fairy lights and Christmas carols. She had a mind to sing and wondered if it would be appropriate. 'Hark The Herald Angels Sing' was her go-to favourite and she beat out time with the back of her wedding ring on the steel-framed bed.

'It's started to snow, Martha. It'll be the first white Christmas in over twenty years,' said the midwife. Her name badge read "Mary" – the irony was not lost. In her drug-fuelled state, Martha strained a smile. Picking up her fallen face from the floor she tried to stick bits of it back together. But she was numb, and her words wouldn't form. When all this was over, she would make the most of the free dental appointments she told herself.

There was no clock that she could see, but if she had to guess she would have said she'd been there for all eternity waiting for the world to form within her. She pushed and sweated and almost gave up, but a promise was a promise.

Where there were two, now lay one. A puff of air between life and death was all that separated them, and she prayed and cursed in equal measure. Pete returned; his face held ash where once was flame. He had been and addressed one nativity, proclaiming the saviour's birth while she delivered the other. Now he was here, standing tall in his shiny new Christmas shoes.

Pete rolled the cot with its frosted plastic viewing window and lengths of cables towards her, and she peered in at the small bundle wrapped tightly in cotton.

Only time would tell if history would be repeated, or if somewhere at the edge of time where the fabric was fraying, a new world would start to rise. Pete caught Martha's hand and rested it on top of the domed cover.

'We need to give him a name, Martha,' he said, his words landing soft and full of feathers.

Martha nodded. In the hours which passed, she watched from the outside as tasks were completed and tests were taken. Her son, her first born, screamed like a banshee at the end of her bed, eyes wide as if the world was already painful and familiar.

'His name is Cain,' she said.

_____

Featured in the *Nativity* Anthology 2019

Strawberry Fields

I never knew my dad. Talking about him made people uncomfortable. They would shift awkwardly from side to side, their eyes looking everywhere but at me. Sometimes they would look down at their shoes. That's when I knew they were really looking down their noses. Lots of people don't have dads but mentioning mine felt raw and unsettling to everyone. I got used to not having a dad. I was seven and would pretend he worked away. He travelled to far flung lands, having wild exotic adventures. Every day brought new opportunities to delve deeper into my library of make believe and concoct new escapades for my absent father.

'Where's your dad this week?' they would ask.

"He's drilling for oil in the Yucatan" was my favourite, although "He's trekking through the Gobi Desert" gained me some kudos with the Year 9s who were studying geography. The crazier my answers got the more I was believed. Everyone would nod and look at me thoughtfully as if it was the most normal thing in the world. It seemed people preferred a lie to the truth. The truth in my house was something you aspired to, not something you lived in.

It was at university that I became "affected". I was off the rails, a car crash waiting to happen. Endless alcohol fuelled nights burned holes into the ozone layer around my heart. I needed to erase you, I needed you to be gone. Which part of my messed-up life was your responsibility? No matter how far I tried to run I was never going to escape. I held onto those made up memories as though they were my much-loved children.

As I tried to obliterate reality – you were off connecting pipelines and smiling at me softly. Each time I got hammered you would run around inside my head, tutting at my recklessness, unbalancing me as I slurred and swayed my way back to my digs. Student support said that my mental health was being negatively impacted by not having a stable home life! Ha! No shit Sherlock! I did a lot of living with my eyes closed back then. It was a safe place to live, I loved my world of half-truth and complete fiction. It was as close to "normal" as I would ever get. I had made you perfect you see. My perfect father, living a perfect life. Only when the headlines read "Child Killer dies in Prison" did I start to really live.

'My dad? No, he's dead' I would say. I would wait, expecting the sorrowful look and outpouring of sympathy. Telling people you'd died sounded good. I practiced saying it over and over. I savoured the words, allowing them to hang suspended in front of me as I practiced looking sad in front of the mirror. No one had ever felt sorry for me before; I should have killed you off long ago. After all, I was not my father's daughter.

Snow Blind

They came for Katia when I was nine and she was twelve. I'd been carving snowflakes with my fingernails on the inside of our bedroom window. The shapes glimmered in the half-light backlit by a full moon which danced in and out of shadows. The air temperature was sub-zero, and the ice was bottom of a glass thick. Fingers numb, and nails backed up with slushy ice I continued happily to chip away.

My eyes were pulled to the street below as three silhouettes appeared to glide silently by. Only one was familiar to me. Katia's small hand was framed by fingers that stretched beyond their reach. Long black talons' rose up and curled around her, the way ivy grasps and cleaves to the side of a wall. She wore no shoes, and the paleness of her feet blended so well with the virgin snow that I couldn't work out where the snow ended and she began. Katia turned and stared back at our house and I swiftly moved away from the window. Her lips were a vivid blue and her white hair glistened, and for a moment I wondered if I'd been dreaming. My eyes drew me back to the window and I watched the now distant shapes dissolve into the crystalline forest beyond. I looked across our bedroom and observed my sleeping sister. Her covers were pulled tight to just below her head, and her eyes were darting rapidly like minnows in a pond sealed beneath waxy eyelids. I paced out the length and breadth of what I had seen but came back toward myself empty handed. I watched the rhythm of her rise and fall, and counted time with her exhalations until at some point I must have fallen asleep.

Morning came, colder than the night before, and our house sat wrapped in a blanket of snow that reached taller than our wooden door frame. When had it fallen? Every word we spoke sounded muffled and flat. Jokes about Siberian winds and Scandinavian winters kept us upbeat. Katia, her face pale and as smooth as porcelain, seemed drained and distant. 'Peaky' mum called it and she filled the bath with water, 'just in case,' she'd said. In case of what I wondered? I was allowed to chop up an old table for firewood – any excuse to use dads' axe. That afternoon I found Katia staring from our bedroom window her tears freezing mid-stream despite the warmth of the winter's sun. Splinters of ice, needle-thin, had already started to freeze her heart. She pulled down her jumper covering her arms quickly. But I had seen them. Long dark swirls danced, animated through her veins. It was as if she was held suspended somewhere, far away but ever-present. A shard of ice tapered from her nose and reached down toward her lap. There was no need for a tissue.

Mum found her rosary and re-instated her shrine in the back garden. Hollowing out an arc in the snow she carved until her fingers became red raw and numb. Dad helped, and made figures of straw, and ice shaped furniture. I designed a small frozen garden full to the brim with icy roses and Michaelmas daisies. The shrine was not dissimilar to our house. Four straw people, three dark one light. Even as a straw child Katia sparkled. Mum hung her rosary high above the shrine. It dangled from a frosty tree branch, 'just in case,' she whispered.

That night the cold bit and tore at us until I felt as though my bone marrow had somehow been sucked out and replaced with the bitterness of an eternal winter. We were becoming frozen from the inside out. I forced movement into my legs and made my way wearily up the stairs to bed. Katia was already asleep. She lay motionless, almost corpse-like, her covers unruffled. Only the frenetic movement beneath her closed eyes confirmed her presence. Mum knelt beside the bed, her soft tears unable to drift further than her cheek.

The next morning, we found a hen frozen on her egg. After that we helped Dad to move the chickens inside, hen house and all. It made for interesting conversations around the breakfast table, and we watched through the serving hatch both horrified and amused as they tore up our small dining room.

When spring came, we moved further south towards Sayansk. Dad said there would be less snow there. I never did see my sister again.

I still look for her each night, but all I see now are large fluffy clouds set grey against the night sky. I remember her beauty, her paleness, her fragility.

I throw open the window and breath in the cool night air. A single raindrop falls onto my cheek and absently I wipe it away. A small shard of ice forms on my fingertips. It feels somehow familiar and I smile.

———————

Short-listed Exeter Literary Festival 2021

Agatha Christie Thinks I'm Grand

Agatha Christie Thinks I'm Grand. Her words carry in the rustle of the trees and the lapping of the river. I walk back and peer out from the boathouse – *that's how people get into trouble* she says.

Her Camellias are in full bloom, and I search along the river bank beneath the umbrellas of green for forgotten pink and white flowers, uncoupled by a passing westerly or a rather rotund blackbird. I want one you see, a complete one, one with a fancy name like Splendid Wonder or Cornelius Candy Cane. One without faded petals or a sunken heart. I want to press it between the pages of Poirot as a reminder of my perfect day in the sun.

It is my first visit to Agatha's house. I climb the track and follow the signs to the top garden. From here, the estuary with its boats, their sails both up and down look picture perfect, and I sway both to and fro, lost in the delight of it all. Sea blues complement emerald greens, and I watch as a passenger ferry cuts through the water like a skilled tailor with silk. The tourists are collected and discarded in equal measure, and they move like ants both left and right. I lose my grip on the perfect pinks, and a trail of petals float out behind me. *Just sunhats and sensibility are what's required*, whispers the wind. The petals arc wide and look like oversized confetti. I am not sure I possess either a sunhat or sensibility but decide it's best to check, and begin to rummage in my rucksack. A pen, a tin of sardines, a tangled ball of wool and a bus pass of someone I don't recognise. I leave the sardines and ball of wool on the path, and hide the pen at the foot of a large oak tree – you can never be too careful, can you? I place the bus pass into my pocket for safe keeping.

I am weary now and sit on a small bench with a hard seat. The mist will clear soon. It always does. I wonder if Agatha ever sat here? I close my eyes and nod majestically; I believe she did.

'Have you had a nice day?' a voice close by asks. It's familiar but distant. He is smiling, and I smile back. His eyes could belong to a policeman or a vicar. Innocent eyes my mother used to call them. In that moment I know I could tell him anything and everything would be OK. He takes my hand, and I let him. We walk towards the gate.

'Mr Luckhurst, your wife forgot these…' A woman with frizz pot hair hands him the sardines and the ball of wool.

'Thank you,' says the man.

'She seems less agitated today?' says frizz pot.

'Yes, she is.'

'Ah, that's grand, same time next week?'

'We'll be here.'

He turns and waves as we head towards the bus stop and I do the same.

Sailing

I need a tag on which to hang my feelings, as if giving them a name will validate them like some sort of baptised disease. But I have only ever been the "tag" girl once when I was on probation, and there was no holy water within grasp back then.

Loneliness is my new disease and my moods are forcing me this way and that like some frenetic push-me-pull-me. My drinking is bad enough, but this brut is visceral. It's taken away my soul, my confidence, trust in my judgement. I've become someone I don't understand, someone I don't want to be. I wait patiently until the house is sleeping, then spreading my wretchedness out like a blanket, silently, invisibly, I cry.

Some days are good. I make pancakes and plait the kid's hair. I lark around laughing at the world and it shines, and I shine back. I talk to virtual people whilst me and the kids dance, and they smile, and I smile too both outside and in. I convince myself that this will be the day when it all changes and the breadth of a day will stretch, and I'll feel alive, and connected and loved beyond the twenty fourth hour.

Then lockdown came crashing into my world without a nod to my reality, my need for routine, my need for structure, and I bled emotions deep and wide. I had not realised how taut, and thin, and long, so very long the tight rope walk had been. I watched as the smallest fragment of me slid away like mercury. My life is now the same swirling bucket as everyone else's except

I'd been swimming in sewage for months. On the surface, my life probably doesn't seem that different; withdrawn, isolated, socially distanced at the best of times, functioning, but only just. But these days I am as different as left and right.

It was always me against the world, I was the one at the controls managing to steer my lopsided boat. However badly I'd listed, I still managed to sail forward despite taking on water. Now, the volume is too high and the controls have become broken. I am heading for the rocks and I can already see despair holding out a hand to greet me. A collective of sleepless nights and fearful prayers move around me, and I awake dizzy and slightly nauseous.

I turn on the T.V. and head straight for the news channels. I listen to the briefings, to the constant boom, boom, boom of the chatter. It's like a daily fix, another addiction. PPE, masks, will they mention the R number, how many have died today? Always listening for the chink, for the "ta-da" moment when things will return to normal – when I can return to my version of normal.

The kids are now at my mum's. The social worker took one look at me from the comfort of her upright dining room chair, and that was that. I used to be called a "functioning alcoholic" but alias that is one label I no longer own. I left my functionality on the table exchanging it willingly for my fifth bottle – it hadn't even been mid-day.

I stifle a laugh and am surprised to hear my voice out loud. It sounds gravelly and weirdly jolly. Today will be the first time in a while that I will speak to real people and it's good to know that at least one part of me still works!

I turn off the T.V. and take a look at myself in the mirror. My hair lies flat against my face and my skin looks sallow. If I squint, I can just about see it, the stillness of the water, the sails set perpendicular against the yards, unfurled and tied. Those times on the ocean were my happiest times, and I try to channel those feelings and those emotions steadying myself for what lies ahead. I purse my lips together and blow. It's time to take back the boat.

I don my flowery face mask and find my keys. No one can see my gritted teeth, but my wild eyes show the level of my utter terror; I'm already at Defcon 3. I remember what I'd learnt at last week's online session and practice my deep breathing and self-affirmations. By the time I reach the corner store, I'm reasonably OK. I'm surprised by the underpopulation; the streets are eerily quiet like a scene from the zombie apocalypse only I didn't get the memo. Quite what I'd been expecting, I can't say and I realise perhaps it not only me that's fighting demons.

I buy a packet of gum, some eggs, and a pint of milk. The bottles behind the cash register are bright and bold and dangerous. I close my eyes and start to breathe deeply again. I can sense the cashier getting ready to press the alarm.

'It's the mask; it makes me feel claustrophobic,' I say as casually as I can, and we both breathe a sigh of relief. It's a half-truth but a good one.

Back at home, I wipe everything with antibacterial wipes and decide to have a shower (you can never be too careful). I phone my mum and smile when I hear the kids arguing in the background.

'I went out today, Mum,' I say coolly.

'Well done, love, how do you feel, Danny, put that down, sorry love, you still there?'

How do I feel? The question catches me off guard, I have been numb for so long.

'I feel OK,' I say, and weirdly I do.

We chat about the kids, about the weather, about Dad and his frustration about the parts he needs to repair the lawnmower being constantly out of stock.

'Bloody Covid,' she says and everything seems, well, it seems sort of normal!

The elephant in the room remains, and as I replace the receiver my hand trembles and I see it looking larger than ever. For the first time in a while it doesn't scare me, and inwardly I smile.

It's six o'clock and I've missed the daily briefing. I flick the channels and find a documentary on Australian wildlife. I make some scrambled eggs and sit and watch the setting sun disappear behind the distant landscape of mid-town.

Tomorrow I will get the bus into the city and see how far I can sail. Hopefully the Zombies and elephants will be long gone.

_____

Featured in the anthology *Aftermath*, creative responses to the 2020 pandemic

Yellow

I walk through the park in my unswerving white denim shorts, tanned legs full on show and looking fine; I'm working it. Me and my girls are doing our thing – slayin – you know what I'm sayin? While I nod along the girls are hollering and spittin', hyped for the night ahead, but my throat is raw all busted and blue, so there ain't no way for me to hit the ball back. I've been screaming on the inside for years now.

'Hey girl, what's up with your legs?' Alisha shouts.

'Ain't had no complaints…' I say but I know she's right, and that actually something's really weird – cause it ain't just my legs; it's my arms and back and belly – my whole body is being weird. But I ignore it and keep rolling to the shoobs with the gyaldem.

The party is lit, the tunes bang and the girls love it. But I ain't feeling it. As I watch, Alisha gets off with Dan and Tash slays with her moves, but all I wanna do is sit tight and sip my drink. I think about mum.

Later, I look at myself in the bathroom mirror and the weird yellow has spread; now my eyes are the same colour as my legs. It's OK, I think – probably just some bad fake tan. But I ain't ever been this yellow before. I say nothing and try to forget about it, I'm not gonna let it ruin a peng night.

Our house sits in its own dump of darkness. That's not unusual, mum likes to sit in the dark. She never sleeps. Just like my favourite denims she's getting more and more faded. I watch her horizon shrink, I say nothing.

I take off my pumps and climb the stairs. Usually by now she would be standing at the bottom giving me that look. Tonight, her space is vacant.

The bathrooms harsh light hits me hard. It burrows deep pushing my retinas into floater alert. My tunnel vision expands slowly, and I root around knocking over bottles of acetone and jars of moisturiser. Mum's tabs don't move, they sit untouched. Just like yesterday and the day before.

I swallow the pain killers, but I know they're not gonna be enough. Turns out it wasn't such a peng night after all.

Some sort of allergic reaction they say. But I know I'm 100% yellow both inside and out.

———————

Featured on *Flash Flood* journal National Flash Fiction Day 2018

He Is Art

He is not Arthur. Today he is Art. You change his name to Arf or Artie or Artu depending on the turn of your head, or the flick of the candle, or the general moment at which you glimpse him. You pay your penny and stuff the candles base awkwardly into the board. He catches on your breath then he is gone leaving a bittersweet aftertaste. The movement out of the corner of your eye, only ever seen in the half-light diverts you. Standing, watching the flame turn fiery red and golden yellow you are no longer sure he was ever real.

He is not broken although his voice fractures as he speaks. Her perfume is woven within him, stitching him up finer than a Jermyn Street tailor. You hold your breath. Only his first three words land, as time slows and his words fade. The moment passes slower than a ship on a calm sea. You resist the urge to pull your fingers straight across his face, catching his flesh beneath your nails. You sit on your hands. Your palms sweaty against the warm leather. They slide first left then right as he turns the wheel sharply. You remain straight-backed and ready to pounce just in case you change your mind. He keeps his eyes firmly fixed on the road ahead. Things are moving too fast. You need to say something. You open your mouth to speak, but your words are pushed back by the acrid smoke that has started to burn at the fabric of your lungs.

He will not be forgiven. You snatch what you can bear each time you gaze into the rear-view mirror. The scars are almost gone, at least on the outside.

He will not be forgiven five years hence when you open the trunk in the loft and find the peacock feather. He had given it to you in the Kyoto Peace Garden. In the dim light, it enchants you. Its eye still stares bright. Mermaid blue fills your vision. You brush the feather against your check and shiver as it tickles your lips. It reminds you of when your world was new before the dark clouds and endless shadows. Your life is filled with a hundred sunsets and still no sunrise. You are no longer expectant.

He will not be forgotten as you try to reach back through the years, clawing away at the shards of metal which hide the truth and which cling to you like a magnet. Your breath quickens. Wildly you examine each memory before discarding it. You try to remember the exact moment before impact. The moment you had been ready to forgive him.

Just One Thing

As the silence spreads itself out like ink on a blotter, I'm no longer sure if I am awake or dreaming. I dreamt I was a swallow once all swoops and swirls but I'd woken up feeling slightly nauseous. This doesn't feel like that, this feels sort of real, but I'm not convinced. Dirty linoleum and scuff marked skirting boards reach out for me and the need to stand up and leave fires up behind my eyes like an urgent explosion.

'Is everything alright?'

You talk as if you know me, but I have no recollection of you.

'Mr. Bretton?'

Ah, yes, that's my name.

'Yes, yes I'm fine,' I say to the small square woman with the concerned round face.

'We're ready for you now,' she says. 'Follow me'

I get that déjà vu thing like I did the first time I'd followed the principle into his office after a fight with Tommy Francis.

'Please, take a seat.'

'Now then Mr Bretton, do you know why you're here?'

At that moment I remember just one thing. My mouth closes tighter than a clam and my words hide and bury themselves deep into my stomach.

'Interview with James Bretton commenced at 07:20 on Saturday May 4th 2022. Now Mr Bretton in your own words tell us what happened.'

A Swan's Path

Ancient trees line the sides of the riverbank and their dappled reflections throw shades of bottle green across the water. Precariously balanced tree roots cling to the worn away banks while the earth around them crumbles and they hang uncertain of their future. The river is in sync with my thoughts today, it's all dark and moody.

My shoes are stuck steadfast in the claggy mud at the edge of the river and my feet squelch and skate inside my soggy socks catching me off guard and I wobble. My arms pimple gooseflesh fashion, and I wonder if my warm peacock blue coat left on the 10.57 to Brighton will ever find its way back to me. Perhaps it is already on a shelf in the lost and found next to an umbrella, or a solitary brown leather glove, dropped by a grieving widow. Wherever it is I wish it were here.

I look down at my feet, as if, somehow, they can help to explain what's going on with me right now, but all I see is the muddy riverbank, cocooning my arctic digits.

After twenty-five years I thought I had this life thing mastered – It turns out, I know nothing. I feel as lost as my coat travelling to a destination unknown.

My thoughts are interrupted by a flock of swans, navigating the waterway. Skilfully they sit atop the water and glide forward. They are like white diamonds, set against a backdrop of gloom. How I wish I was one of them.

I feel the vapour of the mist upon my tongue as it wisps across the water, it's all riverbed and tannin. Now would be as good a time as any I think, but I'm too raw to carry out the wishes of another.

The swans have turned, and are heading towards me. I try to move back but my squidgy feet have me at a disadvantage, and I start to bend from the knee this way and that unable to release my rooted feet.

'You need to be careful, the water's deep here. One slip and you'll be fish bait,' says a vaguely familiar voice. I turn and see a face I do not recognise.

The offered hand belongs to a tallish, middle-aged man. His face is weathered and his is hair voluminous. I can't actually tell where his beard begins and his hair finishes. Perhaps it is a new fashion? Odd beards do seem to be a thing these days. I am conscious that in my current emotional state I could fire off into hysterics at any moment so I purse my lips tightly and will my feet to obey my command and move.

'Thanks, but I'm OK,' I state confidently and with one big pull I manage to hoist myself, unaided, back onto solid ground. My shoes although unrecognisable are, thankfully, still there. I eye the man cautiously. The dog at his side takes the edge off of my reservations. It is panting and wears a silly grin across its pretty face.

'If we're quick we'll be able to get a coffee in the café, come on,' he says.

Without regard for a response, the man sets off towards the café. I don't know why, but I follow him. The dog walks crisscrossed fashion ahead of us occasionally veering off course, chasing leaves caught on the wind. Stealing a sideway glance I study the man. There is something familiar about him. Perhaps it's his crazy hair; it's even darker and frizzier than mine. Perhaps he's escaped from somewhere? No, I reason, he wouldn't have a dog if he was on the run.

The café is deserted. Its tables and chairs are surprisingly bright, all primary reds and yellows. The waitress looks crestfallen. I know that look well enough. It's a look that says, not today, thank you very much. She manages a weak smile – please don't be long it says. I choose a table with a direct line to the door. If he is a crazy beardy man then at least I'll be able to slide my way across the linoleum floor, leaving a wake of muddy detritus behind me! I order us two coffees and the waitress' expression is now one of resignation.

We sit in silence. What the hell am I doing here? A swampy aroma is rising from beneath the table; it's not pleasant. Two steaming cups of coffee are placed in front of us and I watch as the waitress meanders back to her position of authority. More stagger than swagger, I think.

I want to take off my shoes, but I dare not, instead I lift my heels ever so slightly away from their canvas coffins and enjoy brief moments of respite.

The coffee is smooth and comforting and inexplicably it loosens my tongue and I begin to burble. My words whirl, as I share with this complete stranger my innermost, deepest hurts. I tell of birthdays acknowledged, but never celebrated, and of never feeling good enough. My screams eager to escape are clawing at the back of my throat. I take a large swig of coffee in the hope that I can drown them. I have always felt displaced, like a misfiled book in a library. I'm incoherent, but I can't stop. The man listens to my chaotic ramblings in silence. Finally, I run out of steam and sit quietly.

I turn my attention to the man. Cracks and crevices fill his brow and cheeks – he reminds me of a scarecrow; everything sort of in the right place, but with something missing. It is only when I meet his gaze, that I see his eyes clearly for the first time. They are as mine, consumed with sadness. A small tear has formed and is making its way across the fluted surface of his face.

What have I done? I have been so wrapped up in my own misery that I've not even drawn breath to consider anyone else. I take hold of the man's hand. It is deathly cold and pallid. Icy tendrils start to crawl up my arm and I spring back making my chair screech like nails down a black board. Briefly the waitress looks up from her phone, her expression says *Still here then?* before continuing with whatever app requires her undivided tap, tap, tap, attention.

'I'm sorry Nancy,' says the man quietly and before I have a chance to think he stands abruptly and leaves. I feel a stab to my heart; how does he know my name? He hasn't touched his coffee. The waitress senses her chance to shut up shop and is walking with purpose toward me. Her expression is quizzical. She looks at the untouched cup, and then at me.

'Your friend not coming love?'

I'm confused.

'You ordered two cups; I thought you were waiting for someone?'

'But the man…'

'What man? Only you here sweetie.'

Shaking her head, she walks back towards the counter. I know by her backward glance she is weighing up what shade of crazy I am.

My heart is racing. Quickly I pay the bill and leave. I see a familiar shape, dog by his side, heading back towards the river. I race toward him as fast as my legs will carry me.

I survey the landscape, my eyes darting left and right – where did he go? The evening is closing in. The rain has stopped, but the clouds are heavy. There is something lying crumpled at the edge of the riverbank… I can't quite make it out. Please, God, no! Not today.

As I approach, I stare in disbelief. I am shaking so much that I force myself to sit down on the sodden grass. It is my coat, my lovely blue-green, wool coat. Its delicate strands of yarn tickle my palm as I hover my hand across its collar.

The swans have increased in number. With grace and purpose, they are moving slowly downstream once more. Leading the herd is a tall black swan and its beauty catches my breath. There is another, smaller in stature by its side; its red beak gives the appearance of a goofy smile. They seem unusual and out of place, but oddly, exactly where they should be. I catch the eye of the elegant black cob. There is something familiar about him, something I can't quite put my finger on.

I carefully pull on my coat and do up each button. The water is calmer now. I should do it now. Now feels right.

I unpack the sealed jar from my rucksack and hold it close to my chest. If I'd have known you, I could have said a few words.

The ashes are carried by a small gust of wind. They land on the surface of the water and follow the path of the swans. I close my eyes. The pain is still there, but now it's only a whisper.

'Goodbye Dad,' I say quietly.

Creaking

The strongest moments are the ones where you feel the weakest, the ones where you think you may clean break in two and all your thoughts and memories and likes and loves scatter out across the porch and dissolve into the cracks to be hidden forever. Sometimes I hope for that, to be hidden beneath creaky floor boards and to only hear the normality of life continue on above me because then I wouldn't have to hide what I know, I'd be already removed. They'd say *where did she go* or *I wonder what made her leave?* I would be able to keep my secret safe, no risk of spilling the beans and revealing what I know.

If there is one thing, one piece of advice I'd wish I'd known in my youth it's this – be careful what you wish for because one day, when life is breezy and carefree it will come up behind you and smother you with a pillow and as you lie gasping pulling in your last breath, confused and disorientated the penny will finally drop and you'll see with absolute clarity that it was never really what you wanted at all.

Ink and Lavender

Carl

He sits shoulders curved forward over the table. The pen in his hand is held by fingers that are pink and white. His grip is too firm, and the nib of his pen pushes hard onto the paper leaving a deep black a hole of nothingness.

Eyes down, brow freshly furrowed, his expression changes. Words begin to form like waves hitting a shoreline, contract release, contract release. From top to tip his arm holds solid, steering him carefully like a trusted rudder. He writes down a word for every year. No more, no less. Spider shapes begin to fill the page – *leaving, pain, trouble, sorry*. He pauses, crosses through, strikes out, not sorry. He drops the pen to the table and leans back in his chair. This is his third attempt.

He is not yet at peace, not yet empty, not yet rid of all he needs to say. He sits tall, eases his shoulders back and hesitantly takes up the pen once more allowing fine lines and tight curls to beat out freely.

He'd chosen the cream paper carefully. It needed to be strong to carry the weight of his words. He'd had to buy the whole box of forty sheets when he'd only needed one. It was a price he was willing to pay – forty sheets of bonded mid weight writing paper for thirty-two years. It is the only thing that had seemed reasonable. The shop assistant with his tight lips and long fingers had ceremoniously carried the box to the old-fashioned cash register. Carl remembered carrying his cat in a box of a similar size down to the end of the garden when he was eight or nine. They'd buried it besides the lavender bush. His mum had said a prayer, he'd mumbled some words, made the sign of a cross and gone back inside to some buttered crumpets and a slice of Battenberg.

Even now the fragrance of lavender catches him, transporting him back to a different time, a different place. Lavender is a green smell full of earth and wood and he breathes in deeply at its reminiscence. The cream note paper does not smell green, it smells mustard yellow, all bitter and sour. The deep black ink of deceit and the sharp fine point of lies continue to cut at him and form patterns on the page. He counts – thirty-two words exactly. He does not sign his name. He sets his pen down once more and the warmth begins to return to his fingers. Carl sits straight, easing his shoulders back again, hearing them creak and complain like a stiff wooden door. Placing his knuckles onto the table he stands slowly pushing his knees to lock and causing his toes to unfurl onto the marble tiles. He slides his feet back into his patterned leather shoes and feels the remnants of a blister long since burst which refuses to be soothed.

He washes the cup in the sink and swills the cold water around its rim. Its drips decorate the splash back – she would hate that and the inside smile, the one that is as small as a pin head begins to grow.

Returning to the table he folds the page tent-like and props it up against the salt shaker. It is more than she deserves and chiding himself he picks it up and places the letter into his pocket.

The last time he'd worn his patterned leather shoes had been on the hottest day of the year. He'd been returning from a meeting and decided to cut through the park. His feet were tight against the leather as if ready to burst out at any moment. He'd sat beneath a large oak tree and taken off his shoes wrinkling his toes on the warm grass. He was trying to decide if he could get home without putting his shoes back on when he saw her. She was sitting at the river's edge. He watched her unobserved. He was thinking of shouting out to her when a man he didn't recognise sat down beside her. The man kissed her cheek tenderly and her whole face smiled. Carl's stomach lurched. The man was half her age. Carl forced his feet back into his shoes and slowly, painfully he walked home.

That night Carl sat alone in his workshop at the bottom of the garden. He engaged the blade with the wood, moving the plane across the wide length of oak. He hoped the answer to what he'd seen could be found in the now overly worked piece of wood, as if magically a reasonable explanation could be found but all he could see was her face, her happiness her deceit. He couldn't just forget that now, could he?

Maria

Maria touched her cheek. After all these years of wondering, she was relieved. He was happy, he'd been happy and that she supposed was all that mattered.

Maria had two regrets in her life. The first was giving her beautiful boy up for adoption, the second was marrying Carl. It had been a case of right time right place when they'd met and if she could have her time over again her life would take a different path. Gone would be the two-bed semi in Eltham, with the perfectly manicured lawn and the fresh exterior when everything inside was rotten. She imagined a bijoux flat in Soho, a rammed bookshelf and endless laughter. It's a story she's retold herself over and over as months turned to years, until her tears did not fall as readily onto her pillow anymore.

She turns the key in the lock.

'Carl, you home?'

The house is silent. Maria walks through to the kitchen. Carl is at the bottom of the garden, tending to his beloved lavender bushes. Secateurs in one hand, mist sprayer in the other. She watches as he trims and waters his cherished bushes. For better for worse, isn't that what she'd said? She would need to find a way to tell him, and a shiver runs down her spine. Carl did not like surprises especially ones which were thirty-four years old she thought.

Maria walks the length of the garden and rehearses her words.

'Carl?'

'I'm busy,' he says not looking up.

We need to talk, I need to tell you things about my life before we met, I need you to understand how hard living this lie with you has been. But the words stay inside her head, refusing to leave.

'I'll get on with supper, dinner in thirty minutes, OK?'

Carl nods curtly.

They eat in silence, with only the sound of the cutlery interrupting. The boldness Maria had felt as she walked into the garden had vanished and she was back within her bubble of silent screams. She had promised her son, she would need to find the courage from somewhere.

She would leave that night, find a hotel. Perhaps a studio in Soho. She had the money her parents had left her which she had "inadvertently" forgotten to tell Carl about. She washed and dried the dishes and placed the cups in the left hand corner of the cupboard. On any other night placing them left and not right would have been a dangerous move. But she was no longer prepared to walk on eggshells. No longer prepared to mould and bend herself into something she was not.

'Seriously mum, the house was a steal. I think the guy who sold it got divorced or his wife died or something. Anyway, it's perfect for us isn't it Liam?' says Nola Turner looking earnestly at her husband.

'The first thing we'll have to change though is the bloody garden. Who plants six-foot lavender bushes at the end of a garden a few weeks before they move out, we even had to sign a bloody agreement not to dig them up – I ask you who in their right mind does that?' says Liam.

'It's a nice house though. I'm sure the bushes won't cause you any problems, I'll help you with the garden if you like, it can be my house warming gift?'

'Thanks Mum, that would be great. We'll give it a year or so and then you can help us dig them up. After all what's the worst that can happen?'

The Trouble with Socks

I've had fifteen winters to sort your socks, but somehow time had slid silently sideways, and they have remained untouched – black with red, and blue with cream.

Arty said I should've given them to the homeless, but I couldn't do it, leaving them undisturbed was important. They fill the space you see.

At night when fear chokes at me, I peer beneath the bed and know you are never far away.

―――――――――

Featured on *Paragraph Planet* 2021

There and Back – A Lockdown Walk

There – the wind is pushing against my face again. It welcomes me like an old friend, tussling my hair left then right. I feel like a small child with overgrown locks. I increase my stride and my muscles complain.

There – I hear the familiar babble of the water as I descend the shale toward the river. Today there is just air where the fizz used to be. I fill my mind with nonsense thoughts. If I could get under the skin of a jackdaw, or a donkey would things feel less real, or would I find myself still stuck like a broken record, hitting the same there and back chords again and again?

There – a snapshot glance like the click of a camera, all turquoise flash and orange speed. A kingfisher skims the surface of the water and the breath I'd been holding onto is pulled from me and carried away on its wings.

There – I sit on pebbles and my bum moulds to the smooth shapes carved by time. I think of donuts. The high-pitched call of a circling red kite is barely audible above the low grumbles of my stomach. It's time to go.

Back up the hill I walk, and wonder if the turquoise flash and carroty orange were just an extension of my desperate imagination wanting to take flight.

Back against the door I lean and turn the lock twice. I seal myself once more within my bubble of one.

Back I move toward the kettle, flick the switch and hope for the best.

Connect with Nicole Fitton

I really appreciate you reading my short stories! Thank you. If you enjoyed them I would be very grateful if you could write and post a review. It doesn't need to be long and complicated! Just a few words really make a difference and can help new readers discover my books.

What did you think of Soaring? Which story was your favourite? I'd love to hear your thoughts. If you'd like to keep up with my shenanigans please feel free to connect below:

Facebook: www.facebook.com/nicolefittonauthor/

Twitter: @MisoMiss

My website: www.nicolefittonauthor.com

About the Author

Nicole Fitton is an author and freelance writer who has lived in such glamorous places as London, New York and Croydon. She currently resides in Devon with her family and a very sprightly springer spaniel. This is her first collection of short stories. Her debut *All Tomorrow's Parties* was released to wide acclaim in 2015, followed by her second novel *Forbidden Colours* in 2016. She enjoys writing short stories, some of which feature in a variety of anthologies and have been shortlisted in short story competitions. She is currently elbow deep in editing her third novel, a historical thriller, set for release shortly.

Like to Read More Work Like This?

Then sign up to our mailing list and download our free collection of short stories, *Magnetism*. Sign up now to receive this free e-book and also to find out about all of our new publications and offers.

Sign up here:
http://eepurl.com/gbpdVz

Please Leave a Review

Reviews are so important to writers. Please take the time to review this book. A couple of lines is fine.

Reviews help the book to become more visible to buyers. Retailers will promote books with multiple reviews.

This in turn helps us to sell more books… And then we can afford to publish more books like this one.

Leaving a review is very easy.

Go to https://bit.ly/3yFLBje, scroll down the left-hand side of the Amazon page and click on the "Write a customer review" button.

Other Publications by Chapeltown Books

The City of Stories
by Lynn Clement

What goes on behind closed doors? Donna and Jim struggle with an unspeakable act. Millicent encounters something that will change her forever, and Marie dreams of being free from her harrowing life. Melvin's pelvic thrusts have his clients in a sweat, and Sister Francis, the bike-riding nun, has her secret revealed.

The City of Stories is a collection of short, easy-read stories and poems that range from dark tales with a twist, to funny flash fiction that will make you laugh out loud.

"An art gallery full of vivid word pictures." *(Amazon)*

Order from Amazon:

ISBN: 978-1-910542-81-1 (paperback)
978-1-910542-82-8 (ebook)

Chapeltown Books

Short Stuff
by Jim Bates

This is a short sharp collection of well-told stories by Jim Bates who once again brings us some evocative writing with a strong literary voice. We meet a plethora of characters, each with their own concerns and triumphs. They face life's challenges and often have to turn situations around. Will they succeed? Will they make life good again?

In this collections of flash fiction, Jim Bates packs a lot of story into a few words.

"You will not want to put this gem down." *(Amazon)*

Order from Amazon:

ISBN: 978-1-910542-78-1 (paperback)
978-1-910542-79-8 (ebook)

Chapeltown Books

Between the Lines
by Pam Line

The author gives us glimpses into a life full of interesting and wonderful stories. Chance encounters, happy events and tragedy mix into a melange of experiences. This anthology is an attempt to capture truth, possibly somewhat exaggerated, and shows our daily lives in a pared-down fashion, in snippets that appear important with a sheen of incredulity. Most of these tales are true, some even verbatim.

Between the Lines takes us on a roller-coaster life adventure.

"All human life described with a smile." *(Amazon)*

Order from Amazon:

ISBN: 978-1-910542-68-2 (paperback)
978-1-910542-69-9 (ebook)

Chapeltown Books

www.ingramcontent.com/pod-product-compliance
Lightning Source LLC
Chambersburg PA
CBHW081211170626

46811CB00010B/3242